Buzz Buzzard

David M. Sargent, Jr., and his friends live in Northwest Arkansas. His writing career began in 1995 with a cruel joke being played on his mother. The friends pictured with him are (from left to right) Vera, Buffy, and Mary.

Dave Sargent is a lifelong resident of the small town of Prairie Grove, Arkansas. A fourth-generation dairy farmer, Dave began writing in early December 1990. He enjoys the outdoors and has a real love for birds and animals.

Buzz Buzzard

By

Dave Sargent
and
David M. Sargent, Jr.

Beyond The End
By
Sue Rogers

Illustrated by
Jane Lenoir

Ozark Publishing, Inc.
P.O. Box 228
Prairie Grove, AR 72753

Cataloging-in-publication data

Sargent, Dave, 1941-
  Buzz Buzzard / by Dave Sargent ; illustrated by Jane
Lenoir.—Prairie Grove, AR : Ozark Publishing, c2003.
  vi, 42 p. : col. ill. ; 21 cm.   (Feather tale series)

  "Obey the rules"—Cover.
  SUMMARY: Buzz Buzzard comes to the rescue
when his new friend, Redi Fox, ignores Mama Fox's
instructions. Includes factual information on vultures.
  ISBN: 1-56763-727-2 (hc)
          1-56763-728-0 (pbk)
  RL 2.4 ; IL 2-8

  [1. Buzzards—Fiction. 2. Foxes—Fiction. 3.
Conduct of life—Fiction.]   I. Lenoir, Jane, 1950- ill.
II. Title. III. Series.

  PZ10.3.S243Bu 2003
  [Fic]—dc21   99-059547

Printed in the United States of America

iv

Inspired by

the graceful swirls buzzards are so good at. They seem to float high above everything else, waiting to do the job no one else wants to do.

Dedicated to

the small family of buzzards who lived on our farm and kept it clean of all dead varmints. The buzzard is an important part of our food chain.

Foreword

Buzz Buzzard makes friends with young Redi Fox. Buzz has to come to Redi's rescue when Redi ignores his mama's instructions and causes an uproar in the barnyard.

Contents

If you would like to have an author of The Feather Tale Series visit your school, free of charge, call 1-800-321-5671 or 1-800-960-3876.

One

Buzz Meets Redi

The huge bird caught an updraft amid the air currents and rapidly gained altitude. His dark wings gracefully arched into a V shape as he circled the clearing near Farmer John's barn. "Well," Buzz Buzzard thought, "everything looks peaceful on the farm today. I think I will rest a while." He circled the woods for a minute before choosing a tall tree near an outcropping of rocks. After settling down on a strong limb, he ruffled the feathers on his massive

1

body and then closed his eyes. But within seconds, his short snooze was put on hold as excited voices echoed against the serenity of the woods.

Buzz looked down and saw a mama fox. She was sitting in front of her three children and speaking in a firm, no-nonsense tone of voice.

"Okay, I am going to let you explore and hunt by yourselves for the first time. But," she added in a loud and forceful manner, "if you don't return on time or follow the rules I have taught you, I will not allow you to go by yourselves again. Now," she said quietly, "you do remember the no-nos, don't you?"

"Yes, Mama," two of the youngsters responded excitedly.

She turned her full attention to her third child. He was observing a beetle who was waddling across the grass in front of him.

"Redi Fox," she said harshly, "are you paying attention?"

Buzz noticed that the little red fox put his paw on the bug before looking at his mama.

"Yes, Mama," Redi said.

She looked directly at him and said, "Son, sometimes I worry that you don't hear well. Now, listen carefully. It is very dangerous to hunt on this big farm. You must promise me that you will not go any-where near Farmer John's house."

Buzz chuckled as the beetle suddenly squirmed from beneath Redi's paw and scurried out of sight. The buzzard knew that the little fox was wanting to resume the bug chase rather than listen to any ole rules from his mama.

"Redi!" Mama scolded, "Are you listening to me?"

"Oh yes, Mama," Redi replied with all the sincerity he could muster. "I understand."

Moments later, Mama and two fox pups disappeared into the woods.

Only Redi remained, sniffing and digging around the immediate area in hopes of re-finding his prize bug.

"Well," Buzz said in a deep voice, "aren't you going to explore and hunt with the others?"

"Of course I am," Redi replied.

Then the little red fox realized that he had no idea whom he was answering. He whirled around to look for the culprit.

"So, your name is Redi Fox, young fellow," Buzz said with a chuckle. "Well, I am a buzzard. You can call me Buzz if you like." Buzz cleared his throat before adding, "Now, I take it that you have trouble with minding your mama."

Redi Fox glared up at Buzz and snorted, "Nope. I don't have trouble. I just stretch the rules sometimes."

"Stretching the rules is another word for cheating," the buzzard explained. "It is not nice to cheat."

Redi laughed and said, "I am a sly and cunning fox. That does not make me a cheater! Now I am going off to explore the world. Good-bye."

Buzz Buzzard watched the little red fox prance amid the trees until he disappeared from sight.

"Uh-oh," Buzz groaned. "That little rascal is headed straight toward the farm. I better follow him."

Two

Uproar in the Barnyard

Buzz was high above the trees, gliding in a circle over the farm when he saw the little fox leave the forest and sneak across the clearing toward the farmhouse. The buzzard shivered as Redi darted through the barnyard, running as fast as his little legs could carry him, heading straight toward the barn. "Hmmm," Buzz Buzzard thought. "The little red fox didn't go to Farmer John's house, but he is definitely cheating on the rules! I better find a place to

land in case he gets in bad trouble."
Choosing a tree with a high vantage
point, the buzzard landed without
losing sight of the little critter.

Quick as a wink, Redi slid beneath the lowest board of the big corral. A mama cow was standing beside her newborn baby in one corner as the little fox skidded to a stop. Immediately, the mama shook her head, challenging the intruder. She pawed the ground with her front hooves, throwing dirt high in the air to let the fox know that he should leave. Buzz noticed that the baby calf did not move. Instinct told him the little one was in distress, but his attention immediately returned to the ornery fox child.

Redi was within five feet of the mama cow when she lunged at him. He quickly veered away, but her front feet landed on his bushy tail, and for a brief moment, Redi was captured.

Buzz swooped down over the head of the upset cow, and she quickly backed away from the fox. Redi yelped and ran into the barn.

Mere seconds later, Buzz heard the challenging nicker from a horse, a loud crash, and another yelp from the little renegade fox. Before the buzzard had a chance to see the damage, Redi raced from the barn. The little fellow darted to and fro as though he had completely lost his sense of direction. Buzz was having a hard time keeping sight of the little red fox. He wanted to help the little fellow if he could.

Two geese and a duck were resting near the chicken house as Redi raced blindly from the barn and corral. The confused little fox did not see them in time to avoid a very painful collision. The daddy goose nipped, bit, and hissed at the youngster as he sailed over them.

"Oh my!" Buzz groaned. "The

whole barnyard is in an uproar!"

The pig pen was directly in Redi's path as he raced around a tractor and two other outbuildings.

"Oh no!" Buzz shouted. "Redi, don't go through there. Go around!"

The little fox didn't hear him, or he chose to follow his own rules because, seconds later, he was darting among the very angry pigs. Oinks and loud squeals told Buzz that these critters meant business.

The buzzard again took flight, sailing at top speed toward the pen. Three times he dived down over the heads of the threatening swine. And when he saw his chance, the little fox scurried from the pen as the pigs focused on the crazy bird.

Suddenly a truck squealed to a halt in front of the farmhouse. Buzz

watched Farmer John leap from the cab and run toward the front door.

"Molly!" the man yelled out. "What in the world is happening around here? It must be something really bad to cause this commotion. I'll get my gun!"

Farmer John ran into the house as Redi Fox staggered back toward the chicken pen. The old rooster belted out a battle cry as the hens squawked and flew aimlessly around the enclosure.

Suddenly, Buzz Buzzard knew what he had to do. The little fox would not survive this day without his help. He glanced toward the house and saw Farmer John and Molly running across the yard. Buzz shivered as he noticed the gun that was clutched in the man's hand.

"Redi!" Buzz screamed. "Run south toward the woods. Hurry!"

The little fox glanced at Buzz before hitting a dead run toward the woods. Farmer John raised his gun, and a thunderous boom rang out.

Three

Don't Stretch the Rules!

Buzz Buzzard feared for his life as he flew straight toward Farmer John and Molly. "I have to get their attention away from Redi," he thought grimly as he dived low over their heads.

"There's the problem. It's an ornery fox!" Farmer John yelled.

Buzz saw that the barrel of the shotgun was now pointed directly toward Redi. With a pounding heart, he soared low, knocking the hat off Farmer John's head.

"That was a buzzard, Molly!" Farmer John exclaimed. "Has this whole farm gone whacko?"

He fired another shot into the air.

"What on earth is he doing around here?"

"I don't know, John," Molly replied, "but I saw him out by the corral earlier."

"He wasn't bothering Bessie, the cow that's about to have a baby, was he?" John asked.

Molly gasped and looked at John with a worried expression on her face. "Oh, John," she cried, "I'm so sorry. I was busy cleaning the house and forgot to check on Bessie to make sure she was okay. Oh," she sobbed, "I hope the calf has been born and is all right."

"Ah, don't cry now, Molly," the man said in a calmer voice. "I'm sure everything is okay. Come on. Let's go to the corral and check on her." He rested his arm on Molly's shoulder as they slowly walked across the barnyard.

From a safe distance, Buzz breathed a sigh of relief as he watched Farmer John help the new-born calf to its feet. Molly smiled and clapped her hands when the little fellow took his first step toward his mama.

"See, Molly?" Farmer John said with a chuckle. "Everything is fine. We have ourselves a baby calf! It's a boy! I reckon I should thank that little fox and that old buzzard for letting us know that Bessie and this brand new baby needed help."

"That 'old' buzzard!" Buzz grumbled with a frown. "I'm not that old! But I better not press my luck. It's still possible to lose tail feathers to buckshot. I'm out of here!" Within moments, the huge bird was gliding on a strong air current high above the farm.

The flight calmed his nerves, and soon Buzz began to descend near the outcropping of rocks. Two young fox pups and Mama Fox were present at the site, but little Redi was nowhere to be seen.

"I knew I should not allow Redi to travel by himself," Mama sobbed. "He is too adventuresome to use good judgment." As she hugged the two children and wept, Buzz felt a tear trickle down his beak. He shook his head sadly and turned away from the pitiful scene. At that moment he spotted a small object curled beneath a tree several yards from the den. "Hmmm," he thought. "It is against my better judgment to walk rather than fly, but this situation calls for bizarre behavior!" He hopped to the ground and very carefully hiked toward the unmoving body. Little Redi Fox was nestled amid a pile of leaves, crying softly.

Redi's tail was missing a few fluffy hairs, and he had a small cut above one eye. But other than that, Buzz noted, the little critter seemed fine.

"Except for his bruised ego!" Buzz said aloud with a chuckle.

Young Redi Fox leaped to his feet. For a brief moment, his eyes were filled with fear, and then he breathed a sigh of relief.

"Oh, Buzz," he whispered, "I'm sure glad to see you. Thank you for saving my life, Buzz. I really mean it."

Buzz patted the little fox on the head with one wing and smiled.

"You are quite welcome, young Redi Fox," he said. "Now, tell me, did you learn anything new from your 'stretching the rules' venture?"

The little fox looked at Buzz and nodded his head.

"I sure did, Mr. Buzz," he said quietly. "I'm never going to cheat again! Not ever!"

"That's great," Buzz responded as he hugged the little fellow. "And you did decide that stretching the rules is cheating?"

"Oh, yes sir!" Redi said in a firm voice, "And I am never going to cheat on anything ever again."

"Fine," Buzz said, "now go to your mama. She is worried sick about your health and welfare. And I must leave also. Good-bye, little friend."

Moments later, Buzz soared high into the air. The flight was calm and serene, allowing him to think more clearly. "This has been one exciting day. And I honestly believe that little red fox learned the high price for cheating. Wonder what he will do for adventure from now on?" Hmmm . . .

Four

Buzzard Facts

There are two groups of birds called vultures. They are carrion-eating birds. When you look closely, American vultures are similar to large birds of prey, but may be more closely related to storks. Their behavior is similar and they share some anatomical features. Vultures in Africa and Eurasia may have descended from eaglelike birds.

All vultures are large, and their heads are naked. They all have a hooked bill. They feed mostly on carrion. As we know, they will attack newborn or wounded animals. They hunt by soaring and watching for other vultures landing to feed.

American vultures have a well-developed sense of smell. They are a little different from the Eurasian group in that they have longitudinal perforated nostrils without a partition, and they do not have a syrinx, which means they cannot talk. They cannot make any noise at all.

The Andean condor is one of the largest extant flying birds. Its wingspread can be up to 10.5 feet.

ANDEAN CONDOR

The turkey vulture lives in the southern part of Canada and south to South America. It shares a lot of this range (north to Pennsylvania) with the American black vulture. The American black vulture's head is naked, but its head is black instead of red. The largest North American vulture is the California condor.

CALIFORNIA CONDOR

BLACK VULTURE

TURKEY VULTURE

There are seven species of African vultures that we are familiar with. Four of them are found in Asia, and the others live across southern Europe. When the vultures of mixed species gather around a lion kill in Africa, the larger or more powerful species, such as Rüpell's griffon, eat first. The smaller species, like the Egyptian vultures, have to wait their turn. Needless to say, the smaller species eat last.

WHITE HEADED VULTURE

EGYPTIAN VULTURE

Facts about vultures: Vultures belong to the order *Falconiformes*. The American vultures make up the family *Cathartidae*. The Andean condor is classified as *Vultur gryphus*, the turkey vulture as *Cathartes aura*, the American black vulture as *Coragyps atratus*, and the California condor as *Gymnogyps californianus*. The Eurasian and African vultures belong to the family *Accipitridae*. The Egyptian vulture is classified as *Neophron percnopterus* and Rüpell's griffon as *Gyps rueppellii*.

BEYOND "THE END" . . .

LANGUAGE LINKS

Redi Fox needs advice. Buzz tries to help, but Redi will not listen. That might change when Redi finds himself inside the farmyard!

Pretend that you are Redi. People who have problems they are unable to solve alone sometimes write to ask advice of newspaper columnists. Make up a name for an advice columnist. Choose one of the problems Redi created: mama cow, inside the barn, the geese, in the pigpen, old rooster, or Farmer John's gun. Write a letter from Redi asking for help solving the problem.

Exchange letters. Think of a good way to solve Redi's problem your classmate wrote about. Reply with a letter from the advice columnist.

CURRICULUM CONNECTIONS

Watch a buzzard gliding around in the sky. He seldom flaps his wings. What keeps him in the air? Research air currents.

Buzz Buzzard watched over Redi for eight hours. He watched for four days. How many hours did he watch each day?

Form a good habit—good listening in class! Listening is a very important skill, but it is hard to learn. To listen you must be thinking, paying attention, and trying to hear what is said, not what you want to hear. Concentrate on what is going on in class; do not daydream. Remember, you cannot listen if you are talking!

THE ARTS

Build a glider to try out the wind currents on your school playground. See instructions at <www.ag.ohio-state.edu/~flight/build1.html>. Think of Buzz Buzzard when you watch your glider g-l-i-i-i-d-e.... Just for fun, play a waltz!

THE BEST I CAN BE

Redi Fox had trouble minding his mama. He called it "stretching the rules." Buzz said, "Stretching the rules is another word for cheating." Do you understand the difference? Discuss the following happenings. Do you think they are cheating? Why?

Daddy tells you to not pick the first apple because he wants to see how big it will get. You climb on a box and eat the apple without picking it. Did you cheat?

You forgot to bring the math home-work sheet to school that you worked on last night. You copy your friend's sheet to turn in. Did you cheat?

Teacher tells the class to play only on the left side of the playground. You move over to the right side to play just one game of hopscotch with your friend. Did you cheat?
You let a candy wrapper fall on the playground. Did you cheat?

Tell how it makes you feel to see someone cheat. Do you want anyone to have those feelings about you?